# Bubba's
# Red, White and Boom!

## by

## Greg LeFrancis

First Printing, 2022
Greg LeFrancis
LeFrancis Studios, LLC.
4310 East Alexander Road
Las Vegas, NV 89115
www.lefrancisstudios.com

This book was inspired by and is dedicated to our

beloved pets Bubba, Hannah, Amber and Yellow Boy.

"Bubba doggie went to town, to get himself some dog treats. Bones and chews and sticks and stews are his kind of dog sweets." Bubba, the wiener dog sang as he stuck little flags all over the front yard.

Hannah giggled, "Bubba, that's not how the song goes."

"Oh, I know, but this way it sounds much yummier," Bubba said, putting a red, white, and blue flag in the grass.

Hannah barked in alarm, "Where did my flag go?!"

Bubba turned around and gasped, "Where did all the flags go?!"

"Snap-bang-boom!" The sound of firecrackers exploding made them both jump and bark wildly.

"Happy Birthday America!" Yellow Boy exclaimed. "Now, this is how I like to start a holiday!"

"Yellow Boy, was that you?" Bubba asked.

"Me? I just got here!" Yellow Boy said, settling on the walkway.

"Did you take all of our flags and set off the firecrackers?" Hannah asked.

Yellow Boy put up his wings in a shrug, "No, I have no idea what you are talking about."

Bubba went to the pile of flags he had left by the porch and gasped, "They are all gone!"

Yellow Boy looked up in alarm and with wings in the air and wide, frightened eyes he said, "oh no, it's happening again."

"What is happening again?" Bubba and Hannah asked.

"The Ghost of 1776," Yellow Boy shuddered and hid his head under a wing.

"Tell us! tell us!" Bubba and Hannah said.

"Legend has it that every Fourth of July, the Ghost of 1776 comes to haunt these parts. He creates chaos, steals decorations and does anything to keep the festivities from taking place," Yellow Boy whispered.

Bubba jumped back, "well, there's no way that ghost is going to keep me from celebrating! I'm going to put a stop to it!"

"Me too!" Hannah said, standing tall and unafraid.

Yellow Boy shook his head and said, "count me out, I'm not messing with him."

Bubba had a good plan in mind. Whistling the tune, he had been singing earlier, he walked over to the garage and carried the big flag out in his mouth.

"Hewlp me wif dis, Hawnah," he said, with a full mouth.

"What are you going to do with that?" Hannah asked helping Bubba insert the big flag into the holder.

"I'm going to keep decorating. If the Ghost of 1776 is here, it won't be long until we catch him," Bubba said.

Next, they went to the backyard and dragged the large tub for apple bobbing onto the grass.

Suddenly, there was a loud whooshing sound followed by a ghostly howl.

"The Ghost of 1776!" Bubba and Hannah barked and ran back to the front yard.

When they got there, they saw the large flag floating away, flapping in the wind.

"The ghost," they whispered, moving closer to each other.

"What do we do now?" Hannah asked.

"We keep getting ready. This ghost won't stop us!" Bubba said, running inside and getting the bag of apples.

He was just dumping them into the tub when the firecrackers sounded again. Spooked, Bubba leapt and hid under a chair. When he came out, all the apples were gone, and the tub was overturned.

Hannah poked her nose out from behind a tree and asked, "Did you see it?"

Bubba shook his head and looked up at the sun. It will be nighttime in a few hours and the fireworks will start as soon as it is dark enough, he thought to himself.

"We need to catch this ghost before it keeps everybody from having a good time," Bubba said, getting to his feet with an idea in mind.

"Where do you want me to put these hot dogs?" Hannah asked.

"Here," Bubba pointed to the hot grill. "Everyone loves hot dogs; I bet the Ghost of 1776 does too."

They put the hot dogs on the grill and hid under an over-turned cooler. The smell was mouthwatering. Bubba and Hannah had to try extremely hard to stay in their hiding spot and not sneak out to eat one.

Suddenly, there was a clatter by the grill.

"Now," Bubba whispered.

Hannah and Bubba sprung out and threw the cooler over the figure by the grill.

"Let me out! Let me out!" the figure said, kicking and squawking.

"Is that you Yellow Boy?" Bubba asked surprised. "You are the Ghost of 1776?"

"Let me go silly weenie!" Yellow Boy protested.

When Hannah lifted the cooler, Yellow Boy made a dash for it, but Bubba jumped in front of him, blocking his way, "you have a lot of explaining to do," he said.

Yellow Boy sighed, "Fine, there's no Ghost of 1776. I made it all up."

"Why are you ruining the Fourth of July?" Bubba asked.

"Because I don't like fireworks! They are so loud, bright, and scary!" Yellow Boy squawked. "I thought that if I stole the decorations, ate the food and ruined the games the party would be canceled and there would be no fireworks."

"I think I know a way you can enjoy the fireworks without being afraid," Hannah said. She ran inside and came back with a pair of fluffy earmuffs.

"It's not winter," Yellow Boy said.

"These will keep the noise down, so you won't be afraid," Hannah explained. "Give it a try."

Yellow Boy sighed and put them on, while Bubba set off a small string of firecrackers.

"You are right, I don't hear anything!" Yellow Boy tweeted happily.

"Yippy!" Bubba and Hannah said, "Fourth of July is saved!"

To celebrate, Bubba and Hannah put out all the decorations Yellow Boy had hidden. They went inside and got Amber and then bobbed for apples, and ate hotdogs. Then they spread a blanket on the grass in the front yard when it was time for the fireworks to start.

"Bang! Boom! Ka-boom!" Sunbursts of red, green, blue, purple, and gold lit up the night sky.

"That was the best fireworks display ever!" Bubba said as the sky grew dark again.

"Enjoy it while you can," a ghostly sound drifted up to him on the summer breeze.

Bubba turned around quickly, looking for who said it, but did not see anyone. With a smile, he went back to the house singing, "Bubba doggie went to town, to get himself some dog treats. Bones and chews and sticks and stews are his kind of dog sweets!"

Happy Fourth of July!

Made in the USA
Las Vegas, NV
30 June 2022

50936295R00017